MARVEL
SPIDEY
and his AMAZING FRIENDS

A Very Spidey Christmas

Adapted by **Steve Behling**
Based on the episode written by **Robert Vargas**
Illustrated by **Premise Entertainment**

MARVEL
Los Angeles • New York

SUSTAINABLE
FORESTRY
INITIATIVE
Certified Chain of Custody
Promoting Sustainable Forestry
www.sfiprogram.org
SFI-01415
The SFI label applies to the text stock

"Peter, Miles!" Gwen shouts. "Come on, I don't want to be late!"

Gwen and her friends look around the busy mall. She is beyond excited. **It's Christmastime!** And tonight, they are going to watch the Christmas tree lighting.

"I'm coming as fast as I can!" Miles says as he runs to catch up with Gwen.

"Gwen, wait up!" Peter says with a laugh.

Peter and Miles finally catch up to Gwen. They stand in front of a **thirty-foot-tall Christmas tree** with hundreds of beautiful decorations. A crowd gathers, and everyone is ready for the lighting of the tree.

"Now that's what I call a Christmas tree!" Peter exclaims.

"Just wait till it's all lit up," Gwen says anxiously. Gwen's mom has the honor of lighting the Christmas tree this year, and Gwen gets to help. Just then, Peter hears a sound from his backpack. It's TRACE-E!

Peter doesn't want TRACE-E to miss out on the fun. But he reminds the robot that she has to keep out of sight.

"That's really neat that you brought her along," Gwen says.

"Well, it is the **season of sharing**, right?" Peter replies.

Gwen's mom, Captain Stacy, makes an announcement to the crowd while Miles's dad, Officer Morales, stands nearby.

"What do you think, everyone?" she asks. "Is it time to light the tree?"

The crowd cheers as Gwen presses the button to light the tree. But nothing happens!

The crowd is confused. Suddenly, **robotic tentacles** come out of the tree! The tentacles start snatching gifts right out of the shoppers' bags!

Officer Morales and Captain Stacy do all they can to urge the crowd not to panic. They do their best to keep everyone away from the strange tree.

Peter, Miles, and Gwen are just as surprised as everyone else. Using their **spider-powers**, they duck and roll out of the way of a tentacle.

"Robotic tentacles," Peter says. "This has to be the work of—"

Before Peter can say her name, Doc Ock bursts through the skylight above! She is driving a high-tech sleigh, with her robot, CAL, leading the way.

"Ho, ho, ho, everyone!" Doc Ock announces. "Or should I say, oh, no, no!"

"What do you want?" Officer Morales demands.

"Why, I've come to grab some presents," Doc Ock says. "*Your* presents!"

"It's definitely **Spidey time**!" Gwen says. The friends agree and duck around the corner to change into their Super Hero costumes. But first Peter sets down his backpack.

"Stay in here, TRACE-E, where you'll be safe," he says.

Meanwhile, Doc Ock steals presents from everyone. She takes gifts from Aunt May and Rio. She even snatches Captain Stacy's walkie-talkie!

But one quick change later, the Spidey Team arrives on the scene! They thwip their webs and return the presents to their rightful owners.

"I figured you three would show up sooner or later," Doc Ock says with a sneer.

"We're not going to let you spoil the holidays, Doc Ock!" Ghost-Spider replies.

But Doc Ock has other ideas—plus a giant **rampaging** Christmas tree! One of the tree's tentacles swipes at Ghost-Spider. Spidey warns her just in time, and she leaps out of the way.

"Thanks, Spidey!" she says.
"We better stop that tree," Spidey says, "before it hurts someone!"

Meanwhile, **TRACE-E** decides it's best to hide somewhere. But she bumps into a gift bag and falls inside.

The Spidey Team try to stop the tree with their webs. But it breaks right through them.

Then Ghost-Spider notices a flashing ornament on the tree. The ornament has little tentacles on it. *That* must be what made **the tree** turn into **a robot**!

"So," Ghost-Spider says, "maybe if we grab it off the tree, the tree will shut down!"

The friends leap into action. Spidey and Miles thwip webs at the tentacles, trapping them. But the tentacles soon break free again! Luckily, Ghost-Spider glides right between a pair of tentacles and grabs the robotic ornament.

It works! The tree stops moving, and the tentacles droop to the floor.

"Now it's time to take down **Doc Ock**!" Spidey says.

But the Super Villain **escapes** in her sleigh!

"Good thing I'm all done with my holiday shopping!" Doc Ock says as she flies off. Then she sees a bag on the floor that she missed. She grabs the bag with a tentacle but doesn't notice a tiny passenger. . . .

"Oh, no," Ghost-Spider says as the Super Heroes chase after Doc Ock. "She got away!"

"With all those presents?" Miles says. "She **totally** ruined the holidays!"

Just when it looks like the bad guy won . . .

. . . Spidey receives a call over his comm-link. It's TRACE-E! It seems she got out of Peter's backpack and ended up in a shopping bag. Doc Ock took the bag, and now the robot is with her!

It's a good thing Spidey built a tracking device into TRACE-E. Now they can rescue her and catch Doc Ock at the same time.

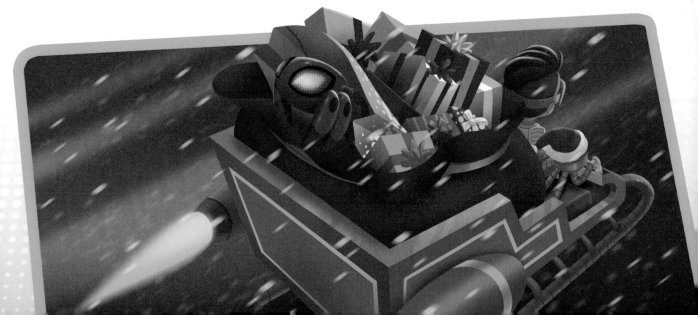

Doc Ock lands the sleigh on a rooftop. She's ready to open "her" presents. But before she can unwrap anything, she finds TRACE-E! "You're Spidey's little bot, aren't you?" Doc Ock says. "You're in **big trouble**!"

"**You're** the one who's in **big trouble**," Spidey says as he saves TRACE-E.

Doc Ock tries to get away, but Miles and Ghost-Spider thwip their webs and stop the sleigh. The Super Villain tumbles out and lands in the snow.

"Well, so much for *my* holidays," Doc Ock whimpers. "I just wanted some presents!"

Then Doc Ock's bot, CAL, climbs over, carrying a present just for her. Doc Ock opens it and smiles.

"A wrench to help me build my evil machines!" she says. "Oh, CAL. It's just what I wanted!"

"Even CAL knows the holidays are for sharing," Spidey says. "Not for taking!"

It looks like it will be a very **Merry Christmas** for everyone—thanks to the Spidey Team!